This book belongs to

This book is dedicated to Paula, Tim, Samuel, Emily and George
A.McA.

To Paula, my advocate, my mentor, my friend –
thank you!
D.H.

This edition published by Parragon Books Ltd in 2013

Parragon Books Ltd
Chartist House
15–17 Trim Street
Bath BA1 1HA, UK
www.parragon.com

Published by arrangement with Gullane Children's Books

Text © Angela McAllister 2013
Illustrations © Daniel Howarth 2013

ISBN 978-1-4723-3181-6

Printed in China

I Love You, Alfie Cub

Angela McAllister • Daniel Howarth

Parragon

Bath • New York • Singapore • Hong Kong • Cologne • Delhi
Melbourne • Amsterdam • Johannesburg • Shenzhen

Alfie Cub bounced through the den.
"It's the morning!" He was ready to play.

"Look," said his mother. "I have a surprise for you . . .

... two new twin sisters!"

Alfie's sisters were tiny and fast asleep.
"When will they be big enough to play?" he asked.
"They'll grow fast," said his mother, "just like you did.
They need lots of food
and lots of sleep,
and lots and lots of love."

Alfie watched
and waited all day.

His mother
fed the twins.

She kept them
warm while they slept
**and gave them
lots and lots
of love.**

"They aren't any bigger,"
said Alfie at bedtime.
"Not yet." His mother smiled.
"But they've kept me busy.
Night, night." She yawned
and nuzzled him close.
"I love you, Alfie Cub."

Next morning, the twins were *still* small.

"I'm afraid you'll have to play by yourself today,"
sighed Alfie's mother. "Two tiny cubs are a lot of work."

Alfie chased his tail.
He climbed a fallen tree.
He followed a butterfly through the woods.

But it wasn't much fun
on his own.

At bedtime, Alfie's mother was too tired to tell him a story.
"Night, night," she said and, with a yawn, fell fast asleep.

"She didn't say 'I love you'," thought Alfie
and his eyes prickled with tears.

"She must have run out of love."

But the next morning, Alfie had an idea.

"If Mummy has run out of love," he said,
"I will find her some more!"

So he tiptoed out of the den to look.

Alfie searched **high**

and low.

He searched **inside** and **out**, over and **under**.

He found a big **fir cone**, a beautiful **flower** and a bright **feather** . . . .

But he didn't find any love.

A big, fat teardrop rolled off Alfie's nose
and splashed into the stream.

Up popped Frog.
"Hello, Alfie! Why are you looking so sad?"
"I need some love for my mummy," said Alfie.
"She's given it all away."

"Hmm," said Frog thoughtfully.
"Well, *you* haven't run out of love, have you?"
"No," said Alfie . . . .

"So why not give her some of yours?"

"Of course!" said Alfie. "Thank you, Frog!"

Off he ran, all the way home . . .

. . . and gave his mother
the tightest, squeeziest,
fox cub hug!

Alfie's mother held him close
and tickled his ears with kisses.
"I love you,
Alfie Cub!"
she said.

Alfie gasped.
"I thought you had run out of love!"

"Oh, I will never run out of love,"

said his mother. "Maybe your sisters
have just kept me too busy to show it."

That gave Alfie an idea . . . .

He hung up fir cones and feathers,
and made them spin and rattle and roll.
The very little cubs watched happily,
all afternoon until bedtime.

"What an excellent
big brother you are,"
Alfie's mother said proudly . . . .

But Alfie didn't answer. All the fun had worn him out!

"Night-night, Alfie Cub," whispered his mother.
"I will never, ever run out of love for you."